GHOST in the HOUSE

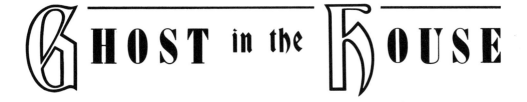

GHOST in the HOUSE

Daniel Cohen

Illustrated by **John Paul Caponigro**

COBBLEHILL BOOKS

Dutton   New York

Library of Congress Cataloging-in-Publication Data

Cohen, Daniel, date
Ghost in the house / Daniel Cohen ; illustrated by John Paul
Caponigro.
p.   cm.
Summary: Includes nine stories about some of the best known
haunted houses in the world, including the Octagon in Washington,
D.C., and the Weir house in Edinburgh, Scotland.
ISBN 0-525-65131-4
1. Haunted houses—Juvenile literature. 2. Ghosts—Juvenile
literature. [1. Haunted houses. 2. Ghosts.] I. Caponigro, John
Paul, ill. II. Title.
BF1475.C644   1993
133.1′22—dc20
92-37858   CIP   AC

Published in the United States by Cobblehill Books,
an affiliate of Dutton Children's Books,
a division of Penguin Books USA Inc.
375 Hudson Street, New York, New York 10014

Designed by Barbara Powderly
Printed in the United States of America
First Edition   10 9 8 7 6 5 4 3 2 1

For Marcello Truzzi

Consulting Anomalist

—D. C.

For Midnight Magic and the Sprites of Cushing

—J. P. C.

Contents

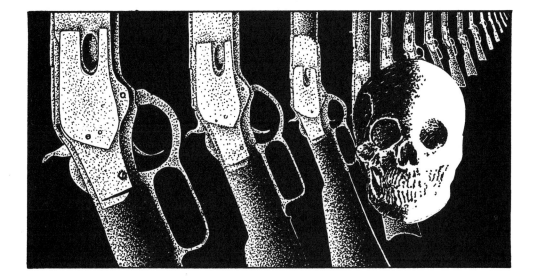

The Winchester Mystery House

Sarah Winchester may have been the richest woman in America. Then in 1881 her world fell apart. Her husband, William Winchester, and her only child died within a few months of one another. The double tragedy crushed Sarah. For a long time she was not able to leave her home in New Haven, Connecticut.

Finally, she did venture out. She went to Boston to see a spirit medium. Spirit mediums are people who say they are able to contact the spirits of the dead. Sarah felt lost. She wanted to contact the spirit of her dead husband, hoping he would tell her what to do.

The medium told Sarah that William had a message for her. The message was that the family was cursed. The family millions had been made through the manufacture and sale of guns. The Winchester repeating rifle was the most widely used gun in America. According to the message, the ghosts of the thousands killed by Winchester guns were out to avenge their deaths. Her only hope was to find a place where the ghosts could not get her.

Sarah immediately sold her Connecticut mansion and began traveling west, looking for a safe place. She went all the way to California. In 1886 she had reached the Santa Clara Valley where she saw a house being built. She believed the spirit of her dead husband told her that this was the place she had been looking for. She immediately bought the house from its owner.

Sarah told the builder she wanted a few changes made.

As she began to explain the changes, the builder was astounded. He thought he was talking to a crazy woman, and he quit the project. The builder may have been right. But there were plenty of others around ready to work for Sarah Winchester, so long as she paid them.

Within six months the original eight-room house had been expanded to twenty-six rooms. Construction continued seven days a week, twenty-four hours a day until Sarah Winchester died at the age of eighty-five. In the thirty-six years she lived in the house it grew to over 160 rooms and covered some six acres.

But it wasn't the size of the place that made it so unusual. After all, rich people often build large houses. The plan of this house was, to put it bluntly, just plain weird. There are stairways that lead to nowhere. Doors open onto blank walls, or worse, to drop-offs. There is an elevator that goes up only one floor. A stairway with seven turns and forty-four steps rises only nine feet.

The outside of the house is a complete jumble. Doors

join windows. Rooms and whole wings are just stuck on. There are peaks and spires all over the rambling structure. It looks like the crazy house in an amusement park.

No one is quite sure what Sarah Winchester had in mind as she frantically changed the plans for her mansion. One theory is that she was trying to keep the angry ghosts out of her house by confusing them. Inside the house Sarah herself wandered about like a ghost. Every night she slept in a different bedroom. When she had slept in all the bed-rooms, she would start the pattern over again.

Sarah Winchester wasn't afraid of all ghosts. She seemed to welcome ghosts of the right sort. Every night she would try to contact the spirits of the dead. Often she would have a formal banquet. The table was always set for thirteen—a number that fascinated her. Sarah would sit at the head of the table. And she was the only one who could see the twelve invited guests.

Sarah lived alone in her ever-growing mansion. She was attended by a large staff of servants who were well paid to

keep quiet about what went on in the strange house. There were few visitors. It is said that she turned away President Theodore Roosevelt when he came to visit. But she did welcome the famous magician, Harry Houdini.

Sarah Winchester left her house for an extended period only once. In 1906 the area was shaken by the great earthquake that nearly destroyed the city of San Francisco. The servants didn't know which bedroom Sarah was sleeping in, so it took a long time to find her. Sarah was shaken but unhurt. However, she got the idea that the whole area was going to be destroyed in a great flood. So she had the workmen build a huge houseboat on her land, and spent the next few years living in that—just in case. But after a while she moved back to the mansion.

Sarah Winchester died in the house in September, 1922. She was eighty-five years old. Today the house is operated as a tourist attraction.

If you visit what is now The Winchester Mystery House, stay close to the guide. It's easy to get lost in such a place.

The Cheltenham Haunting

Experts have called the haunting of a large house in Cheltenham, England, "one of the most remarkable and best-authenticated on record." That's high praise. And it's well deserved. While stories about many ghosts are vague, this ghost appeared clearly to many witnesses over a period of years.

The house was built around 1860. The haunting began in June, 1882, when the house was rented by Captain

F. W. Despard and his family. The main witness was the family's eldest daughter, Rosina. When the haunting began, Rosina Despard was in her twenties. She was a strong-willed and extremely intelligent young woman. She later went on to become a doctor, a rare accomplishment for a woman of that time. She was clearly a first-rate ghost witness.

One evening Rosina thought she heard someone pass her bedroom door. She opened the door to see who it was. Standing at the head of the stairs was a tall lady in a black dress. Rosina had never seen the woman before, and could think of no reason why she should be in the house. The woman went down the stairs and Rosina followed. But she only had the stub of a candle to light her way. Suddenly it went out, and she could see no more.

This was only the first of many, many sightings. Rosina was able to provide a very clear description of the mysterious figure. She was quite tall, and always wore a black dress, apparently made of a soft, woolen material. Her face was partially hidden by a handkerchief she held in her right hand. Rosina observed, "The whole impression was that of a lady in widow's weeds. There was no cap on the head, but the general effect of blackness suggests a bonnet, with long veil or hood."

The figure did not look transparent or otherwise "ghost-like." And unlike the traditional ghost, she would appear at any time of the day or night. She was usually seen only for short periods, but Rosina once watched her for half an hour. A dozen other people also reported seeing her.

Oddly, Captain Despard and his wife said they never saw the ghost. On several occasions Rosina saw the ghost enter a room where her father or mother was sitting. She would point at the ghost, for she could see it quite clearly. She was astonished to discover that they couldn't.

Rosina tried to photograph the figure, but it never appeared in a good light when Rosina had her camera. Rosina tied threads across the stairs, but the ghost seemed to glide right through them.

"I also attempted to touch her," Rosina wrote, "but she always eluded me. It was not that there was nothing to touch, but that she always seemed to be beyond me, and if followed into a corner simply disappeared."

A group of children made a ring around the ghost, but she just walked out between two of them and vanished. Dogs were sensitive to the ghost's presence. Cats didn't seem to notice or care.

On several occasions Rosina spoke to the figure. She seemed unable to answer. Once she seemed to sort of gasp, though no real sound was heard. While the ghost could not vocalize, her very distinct footsteps could be heard, even by people who did not see her.

The Despard family contacted the British Society for Psychical Research. This was the world's number one organization devoted to investigating ghosts. Researchers for the Society talked to everyone who had seen or heard anything. They decided this was one of the best cases of a haunting they had ever encountered.

Who was the lady in black? No one knows for sure. Most believe she was the ghost of Imogen Swinhoe, who had once lived in the house. She had married Henry Swinhoe, who owned the house, after the death of his first wife. The marriage was not a happy one. The couple quarreled constantly.

What they quarreled about most was money. Imogen thought that she should be given all of the jewels that had belonged to the first Mrs. Swinhoe. Henry thought differently. He wanted them to be given to the children of his first marriage after he died. It was said he hid the jewels somewhere in the house. Imogen moved out of the house, and never returned. Henry died in 1876. Imogen died a few years later. But she was buried just half a mile from the house in which she had lived so unhappily. She never got the jewels. In fact, the jewels, if they existed at all, were never found.

People think the ghostly lady in black was Imogen, still looking for those missing jewels.

The haunting began in 1882. After 1886, the ghostly figure began to fade and soon disappeared entirely. However, footsteps were still reported as late as 1889.

The ghost may have reappeared in a nearby house in 1958. The house was occupied by the Thorne family. They had never heard of "the Cheltenham haunting." One October night they saw the figure of a strange woman in an old-fashioned black dress, and holding a handkerchief to her face, in the house. The figure reappeared a few years later. It was several years after this second appearance that William Thorne ran across an article on the original Cheltenham haunting. He realized that the figure he had seen looked exactly like the one described by Rosina Despard more than half a century earlier.

The ghost has not been seen recently.

The Octagon

The Octagon is one of Washington's most historic houses. And one of its most haunted. The name Octagon means "eight-sided." Actually the house has only six sides. No one seems to know why it was called the Octagon, but the name has stuck.

The house was built at about the same time as the White House. It was designed by the man who designed the Capitol Building. Its owner was John Tayloe, a wealthy Virginia planter. The first of the many Octagon ghosts was one of Tayloe's two daughters.

Early in the 1800s, one of the Tayloe girls was supposed to have fallen in love with a British officer. At that time relations between the new United States and Britain were very bad. Tayloe himself hated the British. He would not allow an Englishman to enter his house. There were frequent fights between Tayloe and his daughter.

One evening, after a particularly bitter quarrel, the girl took her candle and rushed up the huge oval staircase that rises from the main hall. She had nearly reached the top when suddenly there was a scream. Her body plunged down the stairwell and landed in the hall.

Did she accidentally trip and fall over the railing? Or did she throw herself to her death? No one knows. But on certain stormy nights what appears to be a candle is seen flickering on the stairs. Then there is a scream, and a sickening thud.

Years later the second Tayloe daughter suffered a sim-

ilar fate. She had quarreled with her father over the man she married. One evening father and daughter met on the stairs. She tried to step out of the way, lost her balance and tumbled down the stairs, breaking her neck.

Visitors to the house automatically avoid the spot at the foot of the stairs where the girl's body lay. Even people who have never heard the story say that particular spot makes them uncomfortable.

Tayloe himself was shattered by the loss of a second daughter. He died just a few years later.

Tayloe owned the Octagon during the War of 1812. During that war the British invaded Washington and burned the White House. While the president's home was being repaired, Tayloe offered the Octagon as a temporary home to President James Madison. The president's wife, Dolley Madison, was famous for the parties she gave. Some of her best were given at the Octagon to celebrate the end of the War of 1812.

Years after the Madison era, guests at the Octagon said they heard coaches stopping in the gravel driveway. There was the slamming of coach doors, and the murmer of voices as unseen guests arrived. Many reported seeing the semi-transparent figure of a woman wearing a turban with a huge feather standing in front of the mantelpiece in the ballroom. That could only have been Dolley Madison herself. She was very short, and sensitive about her height. She wore the feathered turban to make herself look taller.

One part of the Octagon was continually disturbed by thumping sounds. When workmen broke through a wall, they found the skeleton of a young woman. It was said that she was a servant who had been killed by her lover. To conceal his crime, he sealed up the body in the wall. After the skeleton was removed and properly buried, the thumping stopped.

The Tayloe family finally sold the Octagon in 1855. It went through a long series of different owners. Many dramas of life and death were played out there. It was owned by a gambler. He was shot in his bedroom by a man he cheated. The gambler's ghost is still seen there. He is reaching for his gun to fight off the attacker. But he is always too late.

According to some stories, the house was used as a hideout for runaway slaves escaping to freedom. It was certainly used as a hospital during the Civil War. The sounds of sobbing and moaning that are often reported are said to come from the ghosts of the runaway slaves and wounded soldiers.

Over the years the Octagon had acquired a bad reputation. No one wanted to live there. In 1891 the building was taken over by the Sisters of Charity. It was hoped that the presence of this religious group would quiet the ghosts. It didn't work. The Sisters were driven out.

A group of twelve brave, and well-armed, men determined to stay in the house until they caught whoever was responsible for the "ghost noises." They lasted one night, and didn't catch anyone.

By 1900 the historic house was falling apart. It was finally bought by a group that decided to restore it. It is now open to visitors. Since the restorations, there have been fewer reports of ghostly happenings. But there are still unexplained creaks and knocks. And every once in a while someone reports seeing that short lady with the big turban.

Into the Past

Are there places where a person can actually step into the past, and see the spirits of those long dead? There is a very famous case in which this was said to have happened.

The story begins on the afternoon of August 10, 1901. Two Englishwomen, Anne Moberly and Eleanor Jourdain, were vacationing in France. They visited the great palace of Versailles outside of Paris. Versailles had been the home of kings of France, including Louis XVI and his wife, Queen

Marie Antoinette. Both were beheaded during the French Revolution.

The two English tourists were strolling around the grounds of the royal palace. They were looking for a building called the Petit Trianon, an elegant smaller palace where Marie Antoinette spent much of her time. Following a path marked on the map in their guide book, they went through a small gate, and the adventure began.

Suddenly everything seemed to change. There were no other tourists in view. The buildings looked unreal; the atmosphere was very depressing. The two women were sure they had lost their way.

As they came over the top of a small hill, they met two men in long, greenish, old-fashioned coats. They asked directions and the men told them to keep going straight. They passed a small building. Just beyond it was a dark man with a wide-brimmed hat and heavy cloak.

They saw "a young girl standing in a doorway, who wore a white kerchief and a dress to her ankles." There

was a lady in a broad-brimmed hat who was sketching. All the clothes seemed of a different era.

They came to a house, and a young man offered to show them around to the front. And suddenly the atmosphere changed again. The grounds were full of noisy tourists in modern dress. They were back in the twentieth century.

Oddly, the two women did not talk to one another about what happened for a week. Then Miss Moberly said, "Do you think the Petit Trianon is haunted?" Miss Jourdain promptly replied, "Yes, I do."

The two agreed not to discuss what had happened until they wrote separate accounts. When the two written accounts were compared, they were very similar.

The women spent the next two years searching books and old documents about Versailles and the people who had lived there. They came to the conclusion that they had stepped into the past to October of 1789, just a few years before the king and queen were overwhelmed by the revolution.

They identified the men in the long coats as members of the Swiss Guard, who had been hired to protect the royal family. The evil-looking dark man was the Comte de Vaudreuil, a friend of the Queen's who was often at the palace. And the woman in the wide-brimmed hat was Queen Marie Antoinette herself. She often sketched near the Petit Trianon.

Three years after their first adventure, the two women again visited Versailles and the Petit Trianon. Nothing was the same. They found the "commonplace, unhistorical atmosphere" completely different from "the air of silent mystery" they had felt before.

The two women wrote up their experience in a book that became very popular. Miss Moberly and Miss Jourdain were both extremely respectable and intelligent people. No one seriously suggests that their story is a fraud. They believed that they had stepped back into the past. But did they?

Some people think that all the two saw were ordinary

tourists, gardeners, and an amateur artist. A combination of mistaken identity, active imagination, and poor memory created the illusion of the past. Many of us have walked through old and historic buildings and had the feeling that somehow we have been transported into the past. Of course, we are still very firmly in the present.

Was it different for Miss Moberly and Miss Jourdain? Did they really step back into the past on that August day in 1901? We can never know for sure.

The Fiery Poltergeist

The word "poltergeist" means noisy spirit. In a typical poltergeist case, a house is afflicted with strange noises. Things disappear mysteriously, and reappear, just as mysteriously. Furniture is moved around. Small objects can be thrown about. Poltergeists can be very annoying. Usually they are not considered dangerous.

Every once in a while a poltergeist can turn really nasty. And that is what may have happened in the city of Amherst, in the Canadian province of Nova Scotia.

In a plain, two-story cottage lived Daniel Tweed and his family. There was his wife, Olive, and two very young sons. Also in the house were two of Olive's younger sisters, twenty-one-year-old Jeannie and nineteen-year-old Esther Cox. It was Esther around whom the disturbances centered.

It all began in 1878. One night Esther woke up screaming, "My God, what's wrong with me? I'm dying." Her face and arms were horribly swollen and she was in great pain. At the same time there was a tremendous knocking throughout the house. The family rushed around to see if they could find out what was causing the noise. They found nothing.

Esther's swelling went down after a few hours, but flared up again four days later. The noises continued. Other typical poltergeist activity began.

A message was found scratched into the wall of the house. It read, "Esther Cox You Are Mine To Kill."

The news of these goings-on soon attracted a crowd of

onlookers to the Tweed house. The crowd became so large the police had to be called in. Esther herself became very ill, and was sent to live with another sister. While she was gone, the Tweed house was quiet. When she came back, so did the poltergeist.

Now the poltergeist seemed to have picked up a new trick, playing with matches. Several small fires were started, but Tweed managed to put them out before they did any serious damage.

Esther said that she was able to communicate with the troublesome spirit. She was told that its name was Bob, and that it intended to burn down the house. It never said why.

Esther moved out and got a job in a local restaurant. While she was around, chairs were always being knocked over and dishes broken. She was fired, and moved back to the Tweed house.

The Amherst poltergeist became very famous. A traveling showman wanted to put Esther on the stage. He figured people would pay to see the poltergeist move objects around. It didn't work. When Esther went on stage nothing happened, and people demanded their money back.

Esther spent the rest of her life wandering from place to place. She even spent time in prison for burning down her employer's barn. Esther said the poltergeist did it, but the judge didn't believe her. The unfortunate woman always claimed the poltergeist had ruined her life.

The Weir House

The Weir house was torn down over a century ago. But for many years it was considered the most haunted house in the Scottish city of Edinburgh, perhaps the most celebrated haunted house in all the world. Children coming home from school would go the long way around, just to avoid passing the place. They feared that they might see old Major Weir's enchanted staff parading through the rooms.

Back in the seventeenth century, Scotland was a nation obsessed by a fear of witchcraft and sorcery. Anyone accused of these practices faced trial and almost certain conviction and execution.

One of the city's most upstanding citizens during this time was Major Thomas Weir. As far as his neighbors knew, he was a very honest man, and a deeply religious one as well. He and his sister attended church with fanatical regularity. He was probably the last man in all Scotland that anyone would think of as practicing sorcery and witchcraft.

Then, in the year 1670, when he was about seventy years old, Major Weir stepped forward and confessed to a whole series of crimes, including witchcraft and sorcery. He also implicated his sister in the crimes.

The city was shocked. People who had known the old man for years never had the slightest suspicion. While many in Scotland had been executed for witchcraft, on little or no evidence, no one believed what Major Weir was saying. They thought he had suddenly gone mad. And they were probably right. But Major Weir kept on insisting on his guilt. He confessed to ever more lurid and terrible crimes. His persistent and public confessions could no longer be ignored. A group of doctors was brought in to examine him. The doctors concluded that no matter how strange Major Weir sounded, he was sane and he was telling the truth.

Now the authorities had no choice. Major Thomas Weir was brought to trial for witchcraft. On the basis of his lengthy and detailed confession, he and his sister were convicted and hanged.

The case of Major Weir came up at a time when the belief in witchcraft was beginning to fade. That is probably why Major Weir had so much trouble getting people to believe his confession. The case remained famous long after people of Edinburgh ceased to fear witchcraft. The reason it remained famous was because of Weir's house.

The Weir house was a big gloomy place on Bow Street. Shortly after the major and his sister had been executed,

rumors began to circulate. Some reported seeing a spectral coach drive up to the door to carry off the major and his sister to Hell. There were reports of strange lights and even stranger sounds coming from the empty house.

No one would go near the house, much less live in it. The citizens of Edinburgh may not have believed in witchcraft any longer, but they still believed in ghosts. The house remained vacant for nearly a century. Finally, one old couple was induced to move into the place because the rent was practically free.

The next morning they fled, swearing they would rather sleep in the street than spend another night in the place. They said a cow had looked in at them through the window while they were in bed. Just why this should have terrified them is unknown. But after that, no one else dared live in the house.

A book on Edinburgh, published in 1825, said that the old house on Bow Street, though known to be empty, "was sometimes observed at midnight to be full of lights and heard to emit strange sounds as if of dancing, howling, and what is strangest of all, spinning." The account continued that some people said that from time to time the major himself was seen riding out of the alley near the house "at midnight, mounted on a black horse without a head, and galloping in a whirlwind of flame."

A few years later, the novelist Sir Walter Scott wrote of the Weir house: "Bold was the child from the high school who dared approach the gloomy ruin. . . ."

What remained of the Weir house was finally torn down in 1830. The terror the place inspired remains to this day.

"The Spirit Capital of the Universe"

During the 1880s, a two-and-a-half-story farmhouse in the town of Chittenden, Vermont, was the scene of a remarkable series of ghostly events. It was said that ghosts from every age and all parts of the world turned up at the little house regularly. People from all over the world came to Vermont to witness the bizarre events.

The story really starts with a greedy, evil-tempered farmer named Zephaniah Eddy and his family. Eddy's wife, Julie Ann, would regularly surprise her friends and neighbors by making predictions about the future. It was said that she had "second sight," the ability to see the future and to see spirits.

Two of the couple's sons, William and Horatio, seemed to be followed by spirits, nearly from birth. Later, people said that when the boys worked in the cornfields they were often joined by strange figures. They had to quit school because whenever they were around, there were strange noises, and books and other objects were thrown about. The Eddy brothers often fell into trances from which they could not be awakened.

None of this made any impression on old Zephaniah, until he figured out a way that he could make some money off the boys. The movement called spiritualism had become popular. Spiritualists believed that there were certain people they called *mediums*, who were in touch with the spirit world. The meetings or gatherings at which this was supposed to happen were called *séances*. Zephaniah decided that he could put William and Horatio on exhibition as mediums. They would hold public séances. He took them around to various towns where people would pay to hear the strange noises and watch objects fly about, as they often did.

The plan, however, was dangerous. There were lots of people who thought that there was something evil about spiritualism. They believed that the things that happened at séances were downright diabolical. The Eddy brothers were run out of more than one town. Occasionally, they were even shot at. But Zephaniah didn't seem to care, so long as he could find a paying audience somewhere.

When Zephaniah died, the Eddy brothers inherited the farmhouse in Vermont. They started holding séances there. The place soon became quite famous. What set the Eddy brothers' séances apart from hundreds of others held in the United States at that time was the number and variety of spirits that were said to appear. In an average séance, there might be a couple of spirits. But at the Eddy brothers'

farm, there were dozens of different and exotic spirits every night. There were American Indians, Kurdish soldiers, Persian princes, and a host of other spirits who showed up regularly. They all wore their native costumes and spoke their native languages. Some began calling the little Vermont farmhouse "The Spirit Capital of the Universe."

People came from as far as California and even Europe to attend these séances. They might pay as much as ten dollars to spend a week at the house and attend the séances. In those days ten dollars was a great deal of money. The house was very uncomfortable. The Eddy brothers were unfriendly and suspicious. They did not make their paying guests feel welcome. But people came anyway.

Naturally, some thought it was all a trick. They swarmed over the house looking for trapdoors or secret passages. They never found anything, and the fame of the Eddy brothers grew. Newspapers all over the world carried stories about the Eddy brothers' séances.

But the fame didn't last. Spiritualism itself was in trouble. Many, many mediums had been exposed as fakes. Lots of people stopped going to séances, including those of the brothers. Finally, they went back to farming. They would hold an occasional private séance for a few of the faithful. These were tame affairs, at which only a few spirits appeared.

Horatio Eddy died in 1922; his brother William died ten years later. By that time the world had practically forgotten them. Their neighbors, who had never liked them very much anyway, insisted it had all been a fake. They said that the different spirits were just Horatio and William dressed up in costumes.

The neighbors may have been right. Still, there are some who wonder how the two uneducated farmers had managed to fool so many people for so long.

The Calvados Haunting

One of the most violent, and certainly one of the loudest, hauntings in history occurred in France, at a place called Calvados Castle. Actually, it wasn't a castle, it was just a large house. The house had been built in 1835.

From the start, Calvados had a reputation for being "haunted." But exactly what was going on there is not known. In 1865, Calvados got a new owner. The family was troubled by strange noises for ten years. Then, in 1875, things got dramatically worse. At this point the owner of the house began keeping a very careful record of what was happening. When the record was made public, the owner decided that he didn't want his real name to be known. So he called himself only Mr. X.

On October 31, 1875, Mr. X wrote, "A very disturbed night. It sounded as if someone went up the stairs with superhuman speed from the ground floor, stamping his feet. Arriving on the landing, he gave five heavy blows. Then it seemed as if a heavy anvil or big log had been thrown on the wall, so as to shake the house."

Naturally, everybody woke up. The whole house was searched. Nothing could be found.

The noises continued on other nights. Mr. X described the sounds he heard: ". . . some being rushed at top speed up the stairs . . . with a loud noise which had nothing human about it. Everybody heard it. It was like two legs deprived of their feet and walking on their stumps."

By November, there was a new noise. "Everybody

heard a long shriek, and then another, as if of a woman outside calling for help."

In the days to come, the shrieks became worse. "It is no longer the cry of a weeping woman, but shrill, furious despairing cries. The cries of demons."

Windows and doors opened and closed by themselves. Furniture was thrown about. The invisible thing, whatever it was, then began to attack people. Mrs. X was struck in the hand. The mark of the blow could be seen for weeks.

Mr. X's account of the events that took place in the fall of 1875 makes chilling reading.

The family was very religious. They called in a priest to drive out the demons they believed were causing all the troubles. At this point, Mr. X stopped keeping his record, so we don't know what happened.

There are rumors that the noises and other violent events ended for a while, then came back. But these are only rumors.

The Haunted Church

Christmas would seem the most natural time of year to go to church. But there is a tale from Sweden that makes you wonder.

Christmas comes at the darkest time of the year. In the northern part of Sweden the sun may not rise until shortly before noon.

One Christmas morning a young woman awoke when she heard the church bells ringing. It was still very dark outside. She could see that light was coming out of the windows of the village church. She assumed the Christmas service was about to start. She thought she had overslept. She dressed quickly, wrapped her head in a thick shawl, and taking a lantern to light her way, hurried off through the snow.

When she reached the church she found the door was open. The little church seemed crowded. All the worshippers were wrapped in thick cloaks. They all wore hoods. Everyone's head seemed bent in prayer. The room was filled with the soft murmur of chanting.

As the young woman made her way down the aisle, she could not find a place to sit. A figure glided up beside her and grasped her gently by the arm.

"This way, dear," the figure said. The voice sounded strangely familiar.

The figure guided the young woman to a pew, and motioned those already seated to move over. They did. The young woman turned to thank her newfound friend. Then she stopped. The hood had fallen back, and the face beneath it was one well known to her. It was her sister—her sister who had died just a few months ago, and was buried in the churchyard.

The young woman cried out in astonishment. "But you're dead!"

That broke the spell. The chanting stopped and all heads turned in the direction of the young woman. The hoods fell back. What they revealed was all the village's dead, all those buried behind the church. Those who had not been dead long, like her sister, looked very much as they had in life. Those who had been dead for years were little more than skeletons. Those who had been dead the longest were nearly transparent.

The dead began to shuffle and mutter among themselves.

"Run," hissed the woman's sister. "They have heard you now. Run, before they catch you. They will want you to join them."

The young woman got up from the bench and began to move toward the door of the church. For a moment the dead seemed puzzled and unable to move. Then they rose and went after her. Skeletal hands clutched at her dress and shawl. They were not strong, but there were so many of them.

Gasping for breath, and pushing the dead aside, the young woman finally got to the door and stumbled out of the church. At the last moment the hands tore the shawl from her head. Then a howl of disappointment rose from inside. Apparently, the dead were unable to cross the threshold of the church.

The young woman ran to the priest's house. He had just awakened and was preparing to go to the church to say Christmas Mass. When she told her story, he went with her back to the church. It was empty now. In the snow, just in front of the door, lay her shawl. It looked as if it had been torn to bits by the claws of wild animals.

Daniel Cohen is considered an authority on ghosts. His books include *Great Ghosts, America's Very Own Ghosts, The World's Most Famous Ghosts*, and *Phone Call from a Ghost*. He writes about real ghosts. "I don't make up ghost stories," he explains. "I deal with legends and with factual accounts."

Mr. Cohen is a former managing editor of *Science Digest* magazine. He and his wife, Susan, have collaborated on a number of books, the most recent being *Where to Find Dinosaurs Today*. They live in New Jersey.

Raised in Santa Fe, New Mexico, **John Paul Caponigro** studied at both Yale University and the University of California at Santa Cruz, earning a B.S. in Art and Literature. Now an artist and writer, his award-winning work has been exhibited throughout the United States. The themes in his personal work focus on mythology and the natural world. He lives on the coast of Maine in a rural farmhouse with his wife, Alexandra.